THOMAS AND THE RUNAWAY PUMPKINS

By Naomi Kleinberg

Illustrated by Richard Courtney

A GOLDEN BOOK • NEW YORK

Thomas the Tank Engine & Friends™

CREATED BY BRITT ALLCROFT

Based on The Railway Series by The Reverend W Awdry.
© 2018 Gullane (Thomas) LLC. Thomas the Tank Engine & Friends
and Thomas & Friends are trademarks of Gullane (Thomas) Limited.
© HIT Entertainment Limited. HIT and the HIT logo are trademarks of HIT Entertainment Limited.
All rights reserved. Published in the United States by Golden Books, an imprint of Random House
Children's Books, a division of Penguin Random House LLC, 1745 Broadway, New York, NY 10019,
and in Canada by Penguin Random House Canada Limited, Toronto. Golden Books, A Golden Book,
A Little Golden Book, the G colophon, and the distinctive gold spine are registered trademarks of
Penguin Random House LLC.
ISBN 978-0-385-37391-3
rhcbooks.com
www.thomasandfriends.com
Printed in the United States of America
11 10 9 8 7 6 5 4 3
Random House Children's Books supports the First Amendment and celebrates the right to read.

Autumn was a happy—and busy—season on the Island of Sodor.

It was time for the fall harvest. There were shiny red apples to pick. Farmers were busy bringing in the last sweet corn. And the fields were full of bright orange pumpkins of all sizes and shapes.

Thomas the Tank Engine and his friends were being Really Useful.

They took trucks loaded with crops from farms to the Docks and to bustling markets all over Sodor.

Halloween was just around the corner. But first there would be something even more special—the annual Pumpkin Festival in Anopha.

This year, there was a pumpkin-growing contest—who grew the biggest or roundest or funniest-shaped pumpkin? There was a pumpkin-carving contest, too.

There would be yummy pumpkin treats for everyone—pies, breads, soups, puddings, cookies, and even pumpkin candies!

There had been a bumper crop of *really* big pumpkins this year.

The night before the Festival, Sir Topham Hatt arrived at the Sheds.

"After you deliver tonight's mail," he said
to Percy, "there's a special delivery for the
Pumpkin Festival at Anopha." He pointed to
two Troublesome Trucks loaded with the very
biggest pumpkins.

"Yes, sir!" peeped Percy.

After Percy had delivered the mail, the Troublesome Trucks giggled and wriggled. They were determined to cause confusion and delay!

"Now!" called the first one, just as Percy began to climb a bumpy, hilly bit of track.

The Troublesome Trucks uncoupled themselves from the rest of the train and rolled back down the hill! Percy steamed on—with no idea that he'd left part of his delivery behind!

Giggling with glee, the trucks finally came
to a stop on an old siding hidden by some trees.
They went happily to sleep.

Percy headed toward Anopha. He puffed into the station just as the sun began to rise. Sir Topham Hatt and Lady Hatt were there to greet him.

"Percy! Where are all the pumpkins?" cried Sir Topham Hatt.

"Oh, no!" Percy peeped. "The trucks must have come loose along the way."

Just then, Thomas arrived with two coaches full of festivalgoers and their baskets of goodies.

"Thomas, please go and look for my runaway pumpkins," Percy peeped.

"You'll have to find them soon," Sir Topham Hatt said. "Without the pumpkins, the Festival can't go on as planned."

Thomas chuffed off.

"I'll try to think like a Troublesome Truck," he said to himself as he retraced Percy's route to the Sheds. He tried to imagine where two trucks loaded with orange pumpkins would hide—and how they could have gotten there without an engine.

And just as Thomas came down that bumpy hill in the opposite direction, a thought flew into his funnel.

"That's it!" he whistled. "If those pesky Troublesome Trucks uncoupled themselves on a hill, they would roll back down really fast! I'll follow this track and see where it leads."

Soon enough, Thomas found the old siding in the trees—and there were the trucks, still fast asleep. Thomas whistled to wake them.

"Time to get up, you two," he peeped. "We're off to Anopha before you can cause any more mischief!"

Percy was relieved and happy when Thomas returned with the pumpkins.

Sir Topham Hatt was pleased that the Festival could start—Right on Time.

"You saved the day, Thomas!" Percy said
to his friend. "Thank you for your help."

The pumpkin-carving contest was the best in years. And the winning design looked just like Thomas!

"Thomas has been a Really Useful Engine!" Sir Topham Hatt said. The other engines peeped and whistled while everyone clapped.

"Thomas is our hero!" the children cheered.

"And with that great big pumpkin head, he can be the hero of Halloween, too!" James said with a smile.